BURNT TOAST ON DAVENPORT STREET

Written and illustrated by Tim Egan

Houghton Mifflin Company
Boston

www.houghtonmifflinbooks.com/trade

Library of Congress Cataloging-in-Publication Data

Egan, Tim.
Burnt toast on Davenport Street / Tim Egan.
p. cm.
Summary: Arthur and Stella Crandall, two dogs,
are for the most part content with their lives until a fly gets
mixed up while granting Arthur three wishes.
RNF ISBN 0-395-79618-0 PAP ISBN 0-618-11121-2
[1. Dogs — Fiction. 2. Wishes — Fiction. 3. Humorous stories.] I. Title.
PZ7.E2815Bu 1997 96-13720
[E] — dc20 CIP AC

Manufactured in the United States of America
BVG 10 9 8 7 6

For Mary and Reed

It was no surprise that Arthur Crandall burned the toast again. Arthur always burned the toast. His wife, Stella, was quite used to it, and she really didn't mind. It was a familiar smell in the morning that made her feel at home.

Arthur and Stella were happy dogs. They lived at 623 Davenport Street and had lived there for many years. They spent their days doing what most dogs do. Eating, walking, and sleeping.

It was a nice life. Not perfect, but nice.

The only really bad part was when they'd go for their morning walk. Davenport Street was certainly pleasant enough, but down on the corner five unruly crocodiles were always hanging around. They loved nothing more than tormenting the two friendly dogs. They'd shout stuff like, "Hey, lady, what did your husband give you

for your birthday, a flea collar? Haaa, ha ha," and throw things at Arthur, yelling, "Hey, muttface, fetch! Heh, heh, heh."

Arthur always growled under his breath, but Stella would say, "Oh, Arthur, just ignore them, they're jerks." Still, not a day went by that Arthur didn't get furious.

One morning while Arthur was preparing breakfast, a fly flew in the window and buzzed around his face. Arthur grabbed his swatter and was about to flatten the fly when it yelled, "Wait!"

So Arthur waited.

"If you don't kill me," said the fly, "I'll grant you three wishes."

"Oh, come on," said Arthur, "that's the dumbest thing I've ever heard. You're a fly. You can't grant wishes."

"Yes I can," said the fly. "I'm a magic fly."

"Yeah, right," said Arthur, "and I'm a Tyrannosaurus rex. Nice try. Listen, why don't you just buzz on out of here. I won't kill you."

"Thank you," said the fly, "but first, your three wishes."

"This is absurd," said Arthur. "Okay. Um, first, I want a new toaster. And, oh, I don't know, change the crocodiles on the corner into squirrels. And, let's see, for number three, I want to live on an exotic tropical island filled with crazy natives who run around singing and dancing all day long. Okay? Satisfied? Now beat it."

"It shall be done," said the fly as he buzzed out the window.

"Whatever," said Arthur as he continued making breakfast.

A few days passed and Arthur forgot all about the silly fly. Then one morning Stella walked into the kitchen and found a squirrel standing on the counter. "What in the world? Shoo!" she yelled as she chased him out the door. When Arthur came running to see

what was happening, he noticed the toaster was missing.

"Hey, we've been robbed!" he shouted. They both sat for a minute and discussed how strange it was that someone would steal their toaster. Then they finished their coffee and went for their morning stroll.

As they headed down the street, Arthur prepared for the daily
taunts of the crocodiles. But when they got to the corner, they both
stopped short. Instead of crocodiles, there were five shiny new

toasters on the sidewalk. "How peculiar," said Stella.

"Yes," agreed Arthur, "but how convenient." He picked up one of the toasters and they kept walking.

It wasn't until later that night that it dawned on Arthur what had happened. He explained the whole fly episode to Stella, who thought he had lost his mind.

"But it's the only thing that makes sense," said Arthur. "The fly must have made a mistake. He turned the toaster into a squirrel and the crocodiles into toasters."

"Well, Arthur," said Stella, "that's the most ridiculous thing you've ever told me. But if you say so."

"Oh, by the way," asked Stella, "what was your third wish?"

"Hmmm," he said, "you know, I don't even remember. But whatever it was, I'm sure he messed that one up, too. Good night Stella."

"Good night, Arthur."

The next morning Arthur was, well, stunned when he woke up
and saw a ten-foot-tall llama in a grass skirt standing over him.
Arthur and Stella were in their bed on what appeared to be a lush
tropical island.

"Good morning, sir," said the llama. "Grapes? Bananas? Pineapples?"

"Uh-oh," said Arthur. "Stella? Wake up. We have a small problem."

"Mmmm. What is it, Arthur?" she moaned.

"Hello, madam. Would you like a coconut?" asked a huge hippo-like creature.

"Ahhhh!" Stella screamed. "What is this? Where are we?"

"I'm afraid the fly got my third wish right," said Arthur.

Just then, a whole bunch of natives came running out of the jungle, picked up the bed, and started dancing around, chanting, "Ooola, ooola, ooola, ooo." Stella held on for dear life as Arthur tried to

explain. "Excuse me," he said frantically. "I'm Arthur Crandall.
I think there's been a mistake." But the natives were so busy singing
and dancing that they didn't hear him.

When they finally put the bed down, they grabbed Arthur and Stella and started waltzing around with them. Other natives sat around on logs, playing interesting music on colorful instruments. Although it was all very festive and fun, Arthur just kept yelling, "Please! You don't

understand! I didn't really want this wish at all . . . I was kidding! . . . Hello?"

But the natives wouldn't listen.

The celebrating continued for thirteen hours straight, and Arthur still couldn't get a word in.

Finally, as the sun disappeared behind the ocean, Stella had had enough. She spit out the grape that someone had just put in her mouth, stood up on the bed, and screamed, "Everybody STOP!"

And everybody did.

"Now, listen to me," she said. "My husband Arthur and I live on Davenport Street. Somehow a magic fly put us here and we'd like to go home now. Really. Please."

The llama said, "Very well, if it was magic that brought you here, it is magic that will return you to Davenport Street. Now, what reminds you most of this place you speak of?"

"Hmmm," said Arthur, "that's a tough one. Let's see . . ."

"Burnt toast," said Stella.

"Excellent," said the llama.

He took some bread, held it over the fire, then lifted it over his head.
"Now," he said, "close your eyes and repeat, 'Burnt toast on
Davenport Street.' "

Stella leaned over and whispered to Arthur, "Why do I not have
great faith in this?"

"Well," Arthur whispered back, "I didn't think much of the stupid fly either, and look where we are."

So they closed their eyes and began to chant, "Burnt toast on Davenport Street. Burnt toast on Davenport Street . . ."

It was easily the weirdest thing they'd ever done.

Even weirder, though, was that it worked. When they stopped chanting and opened their eyes, they found themselves sitting on their kitchen counter.

"Well, that was interesting," said Arthur. "And if I ever see that fly again I'll—"

"Now, now, Arthur," said Stella. "It was, after all, exciting and adventurous, and it'll make for interesting conversation, if we ever tell anyone."

"And, hey," said Arthur, "at least those obnoxious crocodiles won't be bothering us anymore." They both smiled and wagged their tails.

Unfortunately, their bed was still back on the island, so they slept on the floor that night.

And the next morning, even with a new toaster, Arthur somehow managed to burn the toast again. But to Stella, nothing ever smelled so wonderful.